D1301899

Diary of a Harry Potter Addict

The story of one fan's struggles
through Harry Potter withdrawals

by Anonymous
with Kerin Morataya and Darby Romeo

© 2011 KERIN MORATAYA AND DARBY ROMEO
TWO NUTS CONSORTIUM PUBLISHING
ISBN 978-1463625368

Acknowledgements

This book is dedicated to everyone who has had similar feelings and/or experiences now that the Harry Potter series has finally come to an end. Thanks to J.K. Rowling for her creative brilliance because, despite the ironic fact that she is the cause of these withdrawals, she and Harry have really, really made the world a better place. *-Anon*

We appreciate that this anonymous fan decided to share their story with us. We combined the diary entries with additional interviews, stories and art in the hopes of giving our readers as holistic a view as possible into the complexities of Harry Potter Series End Disorder and the methods available to treat it. Mahalo to our editor and agent, Michael Murphy (Max & Co.), for without his everlasting gobstopper kind of faith we could never have tackled such an important topic (nor afforded the yummy Petit Fortunes™ from the Bouligny Bakery!). And finally, thank you to Alice. As the O.G. Harry Potter fan, you know better than anyone about the side effects of loving Harry and we appreciate you utilizing your instinctual gifts, yet again, and convincing your father to get behind this book project (despite it resulting in cutting short our goal of accumulating as many rejection letters as Ms. Rowling). Harry Potter addicts across the globe owe you a shot of Ogden's Old Firewhiskey! *-Kerin and Darby*

Note to Reader

The diary entries, distinguished through the use of this font, mark the progression of our anonymous writer's experiences, beginning approximately 2005 when the last Harry Potter book was announced and the reality of the series' end finally hit.

Table of Contents

Prologue

Yesterday I recall thinking the world was a magical, whizz-banging place. Wait, was that yesterday, or was that in the long-distant future? The Butterbeer was flowing from taps, chocolate-covered frogs tasted chocolatier, and the world played in a crisp holographic 4-D. But all the glory came crashing down around me, de-evolving into a veritable daily dung heap – was it real or was it a figment of somebody else's imagination? Why oh why can't I... keep the story of Harry Potter going on forever?! It can't end so abruptly – it can't! The other day I bought this diary, because I realized I needed a place to share my almost indecent love for Harry, until I could connect with like-minded fanatics who understood.

Is there such a term as bipolar Potter? Some days I feel like I can make it, but on others the world turns cold and gray and full of the Dark Arts, and my roommate is telling me to take out the trash. How can he be telling me to take out the trash when I feel like dying?!

To recap a little: My journey started innocently enough. It was September 1998; I was a dorky 15-year-old, at the airport store, looking for a book large enough to last through my flight to Osaka, Japan, where I was meeting up with a host family for my first semester abroad. The selection was pretty grim, and I'd resigned myself to the nightmare of reading three romance novels when Harry Potter and the Sorcerer's Stone caught my eye. Although the cover drawing looked a bit cheesy, it was infinitely more appealing than Fabio holding half-dressed wind-blown women, so I decided to buy it. If only there'd been a warning label...

I entered Harry's world as soon as I sat down, and was immediately hooked. You'd think I'd be itching to de-plane after such an endless flight, but nope. After we landed, two flight attendants had to basically yank me out of my seat and off the plane; it was that hard for me to break away from the book. Pretty crazy, huh? (Side note: It's quite likely I helped create the initial Harry Potter fanbase in Japan, having given my copy to my host family's teenage twins, who then passed it on to their friends, and so on!)

Over the years, I cruised merrily along with new books, movies and video games coming out on a semi-regular basis; it seemed like I could enjoy new and exciting adventures at Hogwarts for... forever. But in 2005, a shock was felt round the world when J.K. Rowling announced that her next book was the last in the series. It was like the end of days because the thought of spending the rest of my life in a place so mundane and uninteresting, full of ordinary, boring people, with nothing magical whatsoever became more than I could bear.

To make things worse, I'd get only incredulous looks from Muggles when I'd talk about shopping in Diagon Alley or brewing Felix Felicis... actually, it didn't matter what subject I'd bring up - the reaction was always the same. Like the time I tried to participate in a conversation about Guantanamo Bay's detention center. I thought for sure the wrongful imprisonment of Sirius Black in Azkaban would be of interest, and it was... but not in the way I expected. Everyone stared at me like I had a Horcrux wrapped around my neck, and the snickers started even before I'd finished speaking. I felt horrible. I mean, they may as well have used Sectumsempra on me. A few minutes later, a particularly horrid Muggle offered to give me the number of a psychoanalyst, and I just turned around and left. I started crying the second I got home and haven't stopped since. It's so not fair... I'm a mature adult; this shouldn't affect me. So why does saying good-bye to Harry Potter have to hurt so much?

Now, after 13 years of books and movies satiating my soul, I'm left contemplating either rereading them all for the third time, watching the movies in slo-mo, or maybe, just maybe, finding a way to ease the pain of saying goodbye to Harry Potter.

Introduction

Although it sounds as fictional as the novels that cause it, *Ductor Potterium Serius Terminus Debilitas*, or **Harry Potter Series End Disorder** (otherwise known as **HPSED**), is a very real condition that started spreading on a global level after the release of *Harry Potter and the Deathly Hallows* in 2007. Sometimes referred to by the less scientific term Post-Potter Depression (PPD), onset of HPSED usually occurs within 24 hours of reading *The Deathly Hallows*. Initial symptoms of anxiety are soon followed by feelings of dread and alienation, at which point the sufferer enters an indeterminable period of unipolar depression. Treacle tart cravings and attraction to – even theft of – brooms have also been seen. Left untreated, the disorder can develop into periods of catatonia, uncontrollable pointing of long, thin wooden items at people and, in extreme cases, sudden relocation to Orlando, Florida, sans forwarding address.

Recent research has indicated that the number of fans showing symptoms of the disorder dramatically increased as the date of the final Harry Potter film approached. It is now believed that nearly 90% of fans have experienced some level of HPSED.

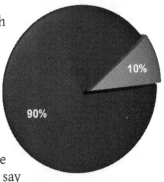

10%

90%

The alarmingly high numbers should not negate the positive benefits of Harry Potter. The story of the boy wizard has encouraged reading in all demographics and inspired fans to become better people. Yet the qualities that attract fans to Harry Potter are the same ones that make it difficult to say goodbye. The books and movies have become an addiction for millions and, as addiction is a chronic, neurobiological disease with genetic, psychosocial and environmental factors, finding a cure is complicated. Since neither preventive medicine nor pharmacological solutions exists for HPSED, treatment thus far has been limited to a variety of psychological and occupational approaches specifically developed by a highly respected group of mental health specialists, the Potternium Remedium Consortium. These have been used individually and in combination to help those who suffer from HPSED regain their pre-Potter grasp of reality and become functioning individuals with an acceptable level of interest in the fantasy/sci-fi genre.

Seven treatment options currently exist for HPSED. They are:

LOCUM TENES POTTER
Once the standard method of treatment for HPSED, Locum Tenes Potter is basically the substitution of the Harry Potter series with another – more often than not *The Lord of the Rings*, *Buffy the Vampire Slayer*, or *Twilight*. Although initially effective, once the story line of the replacement series ends, a new set of symptoms can emerge that has nothing to do with Potter.

ANONYMOUS POTTER ADDICTS
With chapters in almost every country, Anonymous Potter Addicts (APA) is a recovery model not at all similar to the Alcoholics Anonymous 12-Step program. Though beneficial in terms of pro-

viding peer support, the group's methodology has come under intense scrutiny as it discourages any acknowledgement or discussion of J.K. Rowling and treats the characters, locations, and events of Potter novels as real ones.

WIZARDING WORLD FREQUENT FLYING

Wizarding World Frequent Flying has quickly become the preferred method of treatment for the fiscally (ir)responsible and/or corporately sponsored multiple birth families, most likely because of the tendency to overspend on souvenirs. The method was initially thought to work best with a Universal Orlando Islands of Adventure theme park yearly pass, but new data has indicated the opposite. A study conducted at the beginning of 2011 found the method's success rate to be four times higher in individuals or groups on three-day excursions compared with that of yearly pass holders. Researchers believe this is because of the insane levels of debt incurred by compulsive overspending of fans experiencing Potter sensory overload. The potential development of Potter hoarding also exists, wherein a person compulsively digs through amusement park trash cans, collecting Wizarding World-related receipts and dirty napkins as mementos. *(It is highly recommended that this method not be utilized immediately following the Action Potter method.)*

ACTION POTTER

A great option for those looking to get both mentally and physically fit, Action Potter utilizes exercise to alleviate symptoms of depression caused by HPSED. Through intense physical activity, the body releases dopamine and endorphins, which flow through your body, giving one a sense of achievement and elation. As an added benefit, the method usually causes weight loss, which then gives the sufferer a good excuse to go shopping. *(It is highly recommended that this method not be utilized right before the Wizarding World Frequent Flying method.)*

CRAFTING POTTER

Considered the best treatment method for artistic, creative people with severe HPSED, withdrawals are kept to a minimum via crafting projects that incorporate all aspects of the Harry Potter

Universe. Affinity for glue guns, crochet needles, and daily visits to craft stores and online Potter crafting sites are some of the positive side effects noted after 48 hours. A number of individuals cured by the Crafting Potter methodology have gone on to become experts in the crafting spheres of major Harry Potter fan websites, the most successful of those now designing rooms and entire homes for wealthy and closeted celebrity Potter addicts.

ANALYTICAL POTTER*

As with other illnesses, both conventional and radical treatments exist for HPSED; the Analytical Potter method being one of the latter. Considered voodoo science by the Potternium medical community, it is practiced only by rogue, unaccredited psychoanalysts in the Dominican Republic, Laos and the United States. Psychosis and abnormal attachments to pieces of broken mirror have been witnessed in nearly all traumatized analysands. Belief in conspiracy theories and periods of incoherent mumblings have also been reported. A victim of the Analytical Potter method must seek proper psychological assistance to ensure restoration of sanity. Left untreated, psychological damage will probably become permanent and may result in commitment to a psychiatric ward.

LIVING POTTER

This method incorporates ideals found in the Harry Potter series and assists devotees in manifestation and redirection of their energies toward activism through the help of teachers, web sites, group forums, and recovered HPSED (online) friends. Often used in conjunction with Crafting Potter, a person can live in his or her own customized real-life Wizarding World.

Please note: The order of the above treatment options corresponds with the order in which they were experienced by the author of this diary.

* *Inclusion of the Analytical Potter method on the list of treatment is for informational purposes only and should not be considered propaganda or endorsement.*

Chapter One
Locum Tenes Potter

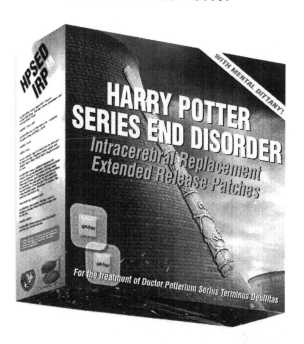

Someone just told me I might have this weird condition called Harry Potter Series End Disorder. Seriously? (Or, should I say, Siriusly?) I know people love to come up with names for every problem and turn them into diseases, but... SERIOUSLY!? I mean, maybe I'm just experiencing something similar to an addiction, you know? And let's say I am an addict... lotsa people go cold turkey to get over an addiction - like the way Willow did in *Buffy the Vampire Slayer* when she tried to overcome her magic abuse (although we know how badly that worked out!). But now that I'm considering it... No, there's just no way I can do it. True, I'm nothing like Willow - all restless and spazzy and itching to cast spells, but that's the only thing I can compare it to - nervous to the core about the impending cut-off of the supply source. A life completely devoid of Harry? No thank you! I wish there was a product available like a nicotine patch. A Potter patch - now that would be perfect! Wait a second... that sounds strangely familiar. I recall reading something having to do with Harry Potter substitution. Is that even possible? I think it's time to Google.

⚡⚡⚡

Until early 2008, Locum Tenens Potter was the most popular method used to treat HPSED. The goal was to alleviate cravings for Harry Potter by replacing them with controlled usage of another film or television series in the fantasy or sci-fi genre, the end result being a complete loss of interest with anything having to do with Hogwarts. Textbooks reveal how replacements were selected:

> "**Beta** females will, more often that not, identify with Hermione Granger. Therefore, a parallel must be drawn between she and a strong female lead character, such as Niobe from *The Matrix* franchise or Captain Kathryn Janeway from *Star Trek: Voyager*.

> "**Gamma** males tend to gravitate toward the personalities of the Weasley twins. Appropriate substitutes would thus include Q from *Star Trek: The Next Generation* or Fred from *Angel*.

> "Admirers of The Boy Who Lived are nearly always **Delta**. It thereby stands to reason that Éowyn of Rohan from *The Lord of the Rings* trilogy, Louis de Pointe du Lac from *The Vampire Chronicles* and Angel from *Buffy the Vampire Slayer* would be suitable character replacements."

Although deemed successful at first, the method became increasingly problematic for what were, in hindsight, obvious reasons.

Similar to the way in which heroin addicts become addicted to methadone, the patients suffering from HPSED became addicted to the replacement series. Within a short period of time, the mental health community found itself inundated not only with cases of HPSED but with an increase in cases of *Buffy the Vampire Slayer* and *Lord of the Rings* withdrawal as well. And with so many new small-screen sci-fi shows developing rabid fan bases as quickly as they were canceled – e.g., *Caprica, Jericho,* – it soon led to a worldwide outbreak.

In the end, a decision had to be made: develop alternative ways with which to treat HPSED or consign patients to futures filled with *Star Trek* reruns and sci-fi conventions.

In spring 2008, the Potternium Remedium Consortium issued its official recommendation against the use of Locum Tenens Potter as a primary treatment method for HPSED. However, similar to fad diets, its conclusion did not prevent people from trying it.

⚡⚡⚡

So, guess the idea is that if I read and/or watch another series, I'll feel better? I'm willing to try anything, so if it takes some sort of temporary distraction like a bunch of angsty teen vamps to get Hagrid and crew out of my head, then so be it. Here we go......

Twilight: 20 minutes in, and the same thought keeps running through my head: "Rob Pattinson was killed in Goblet of Fire, so if he wasn't good enough for Harry Potter, why would he work as a replacement?" And not to knock her, but Bella seems a weak alternative to Hermione. And not to knock the books, but I prefer substance over romance. And not to knock the actors, but I think only tweens/teens will consider them talented. And all this not-knocking has pretty much sealed the coffin. To quote Vampire Queen Bee, Anne Rice: "Twilight's based on a really silly premise: that immortals would go to high school. It's a failure of imagination, but

15

at the same time, that silly premise has provided Stephenie Meyer with huge success... The idea that if you are immortal you would go to high school instead of Katmandu or Paris or Venice, it's the vampire dumbed down for kids." Ouch.

  Lord of the Rings: This is a bit of a dilemma. The movies are a billion times better than *Twilight* (they kicked major, major boo-tay), but the books remind me of this really mean hesher Armando Gonzalez who used to bully me in junior high. And since he loved *The Hobbit* just as much as the album *Bark at the Moon*, I have no desire to touch either one. Which sucks because I like OZZY as a person. Oh well...

  Anne Rice's Vampire Chronicles: Louis kinda reminds me of Harry: quiet, brooding, introspective. I really like *Interview With the Vampire* (book and movie) because he narrates the entire story, but once Lestat takes over... Oy vey! Killing and vampire sex. More killing and more vampire sex. And, hell-o? Ego much? Lestat could care less about other people unless he wants something from them, and that gets boring really fast. Next.

  True Blood: I think *True Blood* is one of the best vampire shows ever on television. Sookie, Eric, sigh... it's an awesome series. Unfortunately, even the pluses (HBO, aka the no-limits-and-naked-people channel) turn into a negative for the ravished fan. It doesn't inspire the viewers to contemplate how to incorporate the show or characters into their lives - at least not beyond fake fangs, blood lust, and sexual fantasies, I mean. Call me crazy for thinking this, but the fans of *True Blood*, they're not fanatical enough!

Vampire Diaries: On the flip side, Vampire Diaries is kinda vapid. Or, as I call it, "vampid" - hahaha. Not to dis its fans because, honestly, these things are all about personal taste (for the vampires too, I suppose). But while Anne Rice loves True Blood, I bet I wouldn't walk in on her watching Vampire Diaries. Tim Goodman of the San Francisco Chronicle staked it in the heart of the matter when he wrote that he disliked the dialogue and hoped the cast of Buffy the Vampire Slayer would "return en masse to eat the cast of Vampire Diaries, plus any remaining scripts." Hear it's gotten progressively better but I'm still doubtful it can quench my thirst for Harry.

Chapter Two
Anonymous Potter Addicts

I was waiting for the bus, and you're never going to believe what I saw! A flyer for an AA-type meeting for Potter fanatics being held every Monday! Fight Club popped into my brain, because if I met anyone there even remotely cool as Edward Norton, Brad Pitt, or Helena Bonham Carter (okay, mostly Helena), I would definitely be distracted from my Potter problems. But then my brain shifts from Marla Singer Helena in Fight Club to Bellatrix Lestrange Helena... and see? There we go again! Everything leads back to Harry. Crap! Still, I'm determined to check it out...

PROCLAMATION.

EDUCATIONAL DECREE
☞ NO. 01

ANY PERSON ADDICTED TO HARRY POTTER CAN MEET US EVERY MONDAY AT 8PM AT FINNIGAN'S PUB

ANONYMOUS POTTER ADDICTS

With chapters in almost every country, Anonymous Potter Addicts describes itself as "a mental safe haven" for Potter fans experiencing "negative side effects of Muggle over exposure." A recovery model in theory only, APA's methodology has come under intense scrutiny by recovery specialists for its lack of practicality as well as its questionable grasp on reality. The group does not acknowledge J.K. Rowling's existence and enforces a strict "no discussion" policy about the author. It approaches all aspects of Potter novels – be they people, places, or events – as non-fiction and encourages its members to do the same in their everyday lives. Meetings are held once a week and usually take place at Irish pubs. Before joining a group, a person must submit a lengthy application and pay a nonrefundable membership fee. This is a relatively new policy enacted after a number of meetings were secretly recorded and uploaded to YouTube. (A lawsuit is pending.)

APA calls its doctrine the "Six Educational Decrees":

EDUCATIONAL DECREE NUMBER 42:
TO YOUR HOUSE, YOUR SCHOOL, YOUR WAND BE TRUE
Never change yourself in order to "fit in" with Muggles. You aren't a weirdo and you're not alone in your love of Harry Potter. Like-minded individuals exist, and you'll always find a seat at a house table in the Great Hall.

EDUCATIONAL DECREE NUMBER 87:
MISCHIEF MUST ALWAYS BE MANAGED
Use moderation when playing tricks on others. Too much Draco-like behavior can get you punched.

EDUCATIONAL DECREE NUMBER 11:
NEVER UNDERESTIMATE THE POWER OF A BOW
Be polite even in the most trying of circumstances. Civility can turn a wary, aloof Hippogriff into a very loyal and affectionate ally.

EDUCATIONAL DECREE NUMBER 3:
DO NOT FEAR A CHANGED PATRONUS
Although changes in emotional support systems often occur, your trust in the Harry Potter community will always guarantee at least one person to lean on.

EDUCATIONAL DECREE NUMBER 20:
DO NOT FORGO THE CASTING OF AN UNFORGIVABLE CURSE
In circumstances of life or death, taking extreme measures may be

the only option for survival. If you are in reasonable fear of serious injury or death, do not hesitate to cast.

EDUCATIONAL DECREE NUMBER 108:
WHEN FACING A DAUNTING CHALLENGE, ASK "WHAT WOULD HARRY POTTER DO?"
Whether it be Harry Potter, Hermione Granger, Severus Snape, or the Weasley Twins, you will find a role model at Hogwarts. Their strengths and weaknesses, successes and failures, can help you find a way out of life's trickiest mazes.

The APA meetings were kinda cool at first - or should I say entertaining? Instead of Edward, Brad, and Helena, there was Ted (a misplaced Hagrid-looking Hobbit geek... from, like, the '70s!), Gina (an English lady whose problems included acting out the parts of every mature female character in H.P. - and who eventually got booted for admitting she thought she was J.K.!), as well as a skinny metal-head named Boris (who complained every single meeting that he was supposed to have been cast in the first film but he'd caught the flu). Besides that, there was a loose group of ne'er-do-well wannabes who might have been too wasted to find the NA meeting - none of them interesting enough to make me want to try heroin, that's for sure. Onward.

Chapter Three
Wizarding World Frequent Flying

```
BUTTERBEER REFILL        3.99

       SUBTOTAL          3.99
       SALES TAX          .30

   TOTAL                 4.29


THANK YOU FOR SPENDING
  YOUR GOLD WITH US!
```

Even though it's taken me forever to save up enough money to do it, and even though I've had to go without WoW, Second Life, and Hot Chicks With Glasses for almost a year, it's finally happening — I'LL BE AT WIZARDING WORLD TOMORROW!!

I've never been this excited about anything in my life. I'm going on the Forbidden Journey first because it sounds incredible, and I can't think of a more appropriate way to start my visit than with a tour of Hogwarts. I think I'm gonna hit Ollivanders next. There's been a lot of talk on the Internet about the long lines to get in, but that OBVIOUSLY means it's worth the wait (and I'm determined to get picked for the wand choosing, too!). I'll definitely need to get my sugar on afterward, so a visit to Honeydukes comes next and then... who knows? And who cares? All that matters is that I'LL BE AT WIZARDING WORLD TOMORROW!!

I'm so happy about my trip that I'm not gonna spend any time worrying about getting laid off this afternoon. I budgeted everything perfectly. I mean, it's not like I'm going to buy a million dollars worth of Harry Potter t-shirts, right? Hahahaha! And you never know... maybe I'll find a new job while I'm there!

Orlando, here I come!!!

DAY ONE

Incredible, awesome, beyond anything I ever imagined... Wizarding World is a Harry Potter fan's heaven. Well, at least for me it is! Definitely overspent at Honeydukes, but since I can't think of another place that sells chocolate frogs, I decided to stock up. No big deal — I just won't buy any more fudge flies!

So wiped out! The lines were pretty long, so my feet are hurting a little. Think I'm going to order dinner and then turn in for the night. I want to be the first Muggle to get in tomorrow morning!

DAY TWO

Although my second day at Wizarding World started wonderfully and deliciously

CHOCOLATE FROG	9.95
CHOCOLATE FROG	9.95
CHOCOLATE FROG	9.95
CHOCOLATE FROG	9.95
CHOCOLATE FROG	9.95
TON TONGUE TOFFEE	12.95
BERNIE BOTT'S EVERY FLAVOR BEANS BAG	8.95
BERNIE BOTT'S EVERY FLAVOR BEANS BOX	11.95
HONEYDUKE'S ACID POP	3.95
HONEYDUKE'S ACID POP	3.95
PUMPKIN JUICE	5.95
PUMPKIN JUICE	5.95
DARK MARK LOLLIPOP	3.95
TONGUE BURNERS TOOTH SPLINTERING MINTS	4.95
CANARY CREMES	9.95
FUDGE FLIES	6.95
SCREAMING YO YO	9.95
SNEAKOSCOPE	14.95
CHOCOLATE WAND	5.95
CHOCOLATE CAULDRON	9.95
WHITE CHOCOLATE SKULLS	9.95
SUBTOTAL	179.95
SALES TAX	11.70
TOTAL	191.65

THANK YOU FOR SPENDING
YOUR GOLD WITH US!

YOUR PURCHASE EARNED YOU
1,700 WIZARDING POINTS!

enough... things kinda got out of hand at the end. UGGGHHH! How on Earth did I spend over $1,600.00 in ONE day?!? After all that scrimping and saving and careful budgeting, how could I have been so stupid and irresponsible? The only logical explanation is that someone put me under the Imperius Curse. Seriously, because I would never have done it had I been in my right mind. Unfortunately, there's no way to reverse the damage my actions have caused, and I'm very, very afraid of what lies ahead.

At least there's a silver lining to the whole mess... I had a great day. Arrived early and was able to ride Dragon Challenge before the line got too long.

Next, I went to Ollivanders, but was kicked out before the show started because I scared people by... hissing and mumbling incoherently. Or at least that's what I was told by the security guards. I don't remember doing it,

RAVENCLAW ROBE	
RAVENCLAW SCARF	99.95
CHINESE FIREBALL	34.95
DRAGON PLUSH TOY	
OMNIOCULARS	21.95
LARGE CAULDRON	34.95
BLUDGER BAT & BALL SET	34.95
FIREBOLT BROOM	21.95
HOGWARTS JOURNAL	299.95
GOLDEN SNITCH	21.95
WIZARD CHESS SET	14.95
DEATH EATER MASK	899.95
HEDWIG PUPPET W/SOUND	99.95
DELUXE MAURAUDER'S MAP	29.95
VOLDEMORT PLUSH TOY	64.95
PYGMY PUFF	24.95
HERMIONE WAND	12.95
SEVERUS SNAPE WAND	28.95
DA KEYCHAIN	28.95
TRIWIZARD CHAMPIONS	7.95
WAND COLLECTION	
TIME TURNER NECKLACE	119.95
COMB-A-CHAMELEON	64.95
	9.95
SUBTOTAL	1,374.10
SALES TAX	89.32
TOTAL	1,463.42

THANK YOU FOR SPENDING YOUR GOLD WITH US!

YOUR PURCHASE EARNED YOU 15,000 WIZARDING POINTS!

but maybe I was actually speaking Parseltongue? I apologized profusely, and security was very nice about it. One of them even mentioned that the sun had probably gotten to me and that it'd happened to a few other guests since the park had opened, so maybe the idea that I'm a closet Parselmouth is not so far-fetched.

Anyway, I didn't bother getting back in line because I was super hungry by that point, so I went to the Three Broomsticks and totally pigged out. Didn't intend to buy so much food, but everything looked sooo good — ordered almost everything on the menu! And although it might sound ridiculous to have spent so much on eats, I did save the leftovers for the remainder of my trip, and I'm pretty certain I'll end up bringing some home with me, too; a good thing since I'm not sure when I'll be able to afford groceries again.

```
GREAT FEAST             49.99
SHEPHERD'S PIE           9.99
FISH/CHIPS              11.99
FRZN BUTTERBEER W/MUG    8.50

  SUBTOTAL              80.47
  SALES TAX              5.23
  GRATUITY (20%)        17.14

  TOTAL                102.85
```

THANK YOU FOR SPENDING
YOUR GOLD WITH US!

YOU'VE EARNED A FREE MEAL
FOR YOUR NEXT VISIT!
(FREE MEAL EXCLUDES THE GREAT FEAST)

So, after indulging, I wanted to check out Ollivanders again, but since the line was super long when I got there, I popped into the Owl Post instead (right next door). I'd read on the internet that everything mailed from the Owl Post gets stamped with a really cool Hogsmeade postmark, so I sent one to a friend and to myself. Checked the line again for Ollivanders and, since it wasn't any shorter, I went into Dervish and Banges (also right next door). That's when disaster hit. Ninety minutes later, completely confounded, I literally staggered out of the shop with pretty much its entire inventory. It wasn't until I got back to the hotel that it hit me what had happened.

OOOMMMMGGG. I just checked the receipt again, for the tenth time – returns are definitely not accepted. Bloody hell! What am I going to do?!?

DAY THREE
The fact that listening to the Frog Choir while drinking a butterbeer did nothing to cheer me up, and makes this one of the worst days ever. What a terrible way to end my trip – but it was so much fun!

THE AFTERMATH
Splinch me. Splinch me now.

ONLINE BANKING STATEMENT

TYPE

Cash & Credit

Investment

ACCOUNTS edit

All Accounts
1 accounts

Q [   ] **Search**

All Cash & Credit Accounts

TOTAL CASH $1,700.00   **TOTAL DEBT** $2,778.03

☑ Edit Multiple   ✚ Add a Transaction

	Date ▼	Description	Category	Amount
☐	SEP 13	BALANCE	--------- ▼	-2778.03
☐	SEP 13	RETURNED CHECK FEES (4) EDIT DETAILS	FEES	-200.00
☐	SEP 13	OVERDRAFT FEES (6)	FEES	-222.00
☐	SEP 13	NATIONAL GAS & POWER	GAS/ELECTRIC	-58.43
☐	SEP 13	PACBELL	PHONE	-157.24
☐	SEP 13	MACALLY PROPERTIES, INC.	RENT	-850.00
☐	SEP 13	GEICO	CAR INSURANCE	-45.00
☐	SEP 12	WIZARDING WORLD	MISC	-4.29
☐	SEP 12	MINI-BAR CHARGE	ALCOHOL	-11.50
☐	SEP 11	WIZARDING WORLD	MISC	4.29
☐	SEP 11	WIZARDING WORLD	MISC	4.29
☐	SEP 11	WIZARDING WORLD	MISC	102.85
☐	SEP 11	WIZARDING WORLD	MISC	-1575.08
☐	SEP 11	MINI-BAR CHARGE	ALCOHOL	-11.50
☐	SEP 11	MINI-BAR CHARGE	ALCOHOL	-11.50
☐	SEP 11	MINI-BAR CHARGE	ALCOHOL	-11.50
☐	SEP 10	WIZARDING WORLD	MISC	4.29
☐	SEP 10	WIZARDING WORLD	MISC	4.29
☐	SEP 10	WIZARDING WORLD	MISC	191.65
☐	SEP 10	ROOM SERVICE	FOOD	32.00
☐	SEP 10	MINI-BAR CHARGE	ALCOHOL	11.50
☐	SEP 10	MINI-BAR CHARGE	ALCOHOL	11.50
☐	SEP 10	ON-DEMAND CHANNEL	ENTERTAINMENT	9.00
☐	SEP 09	AUTOMATIC DEPOSIT	INCOME	1700.00
☐	SEP 09	EL MEJOR CAR RENTAL	TRAVEL	76.68
☐	SEP 09	UNITED AIRLINES	TRAVEL	638.65
☐	SEP 09	UNIVERSAL STUDIOS ORLANDO	TRAVEL	239.00

Chapter Four
Action Potter

I feel like I was chained to a pair of Dementors the second I left Wizarding World. Living with Muggles was hard enough before my trip, but now... now, I'm struggling just to get out of bed. Nothing I've done has had any impact — my life will never be the same without Harry, so what's the point of getting up? I feel so lost and alone, so empty and miserable (okay, maybe it's partly because I just spent this month's rent on my Wizarding World trip).

If Cadmus Peverall felt even a little like I do now, then he had the right idea. I said that to a friend last night. She's pretty much the only friend that lets me be me (although she doesn't understand half of what I'm talking about, she's kind enough to listen and not make me feel like a freak). Anyway, after I told her "The Tale of The Three Brothers" (she obviously had no idea who Cadmus Peverall was) she said she had to go home. She insisted it was because she had something that might cheer me up, but I didn't believe her; I just assumed that I'd finally scared her off. So when I got an email from her a few hours later, my mind was completely blown.

She had come across a story on the Internet about a Muggle Quidditch team. Sounds totally fake, right? Well, it did to her, and since she wanted to make sure it was real before she told me, she did some more research – and guess what? It's true! There's an actual LEAGUE. The International Quidditch Association. There are teams in almost every state – in other countries even – and more are being formed all the time. My friend found one at a nearby college, and we're going to a match today. Even though I'm trying not to get my hopes up, I'm really, really excited. Muggle Quidditch! I still can't believe it!

It is difficult to find the motivation to move when you're depressed – lying in bed can definitely be more appealing than running laps. But over the past two decades, studies have concluded that exercise can improve moods in people with mild to moderate depression. It also may play a supporting role in treating severe depression.

How does exercise relieve depression? For many years, experts have known that exercise enhances the action of endorphins, chemicals that circulate throughout the body. Endorphins improve natural immunity and reduce the perception of pain. They may also serve to improve mood. Another theory is that exercise stimulates the neurotransmitter norepinephrine, which may directly improve mood. How often or intensely you need to exercise to alleviate depression is not clear; but for general health, experts advise getting half an hour to an hour of moderate exercise, such as brisk walking, on all or most days of the week.

If the idea of playing real-life Quidditch is not appealing, fencing may be an answer. Check local college or community centers to see if classes are offered, or find a private trainer. Another option that works both the brain and the body is designing a garden maze for a personal Triwizard Tournament. The maze can be easy, as fake plants or plywood covered with astro-turf can be used instead of hedges. Muggle Quidditch, however, is the obvious ideal solution for dealing with depression caused by HPSED.

"It's a great sport that gets you out there exercising and interacting positively with others, all while making a connection to your favorite book series."

Alicia Radford of

International Quidditch Association

According to *Quidditch Through the Ages*, the 700 potential fouls in Quidditch have never been made available to the public. How, then, do refs know when one is committed? Is there a place where these rules are kept? Do official refs gain access, and if so, are non-disclosure agreements used?

While we love the book *Quidditch Through the Ages* and think it's a great addition to the Harry Potter canon, the rules of IQA Quidditch are based on the simple rules of Quidditch in the Harry Potter series. Beyond that, our fouls and rules have developed based on what is dangerous to our new sport – for example, players are not allowed to trip one another, or do two-handed tackles, because they are dangerous. Some fouls are the same as in the Harry Potter books – players aren't allowed to grab on to another's cape or broomstick – but others are necessarily different because of our different playing conditions. All of our fouls and physical contact rules are available in our rulebook, and refs and players are expected to know them, as in other sports. Otherwise it would be dangerous and unfair!

Are there any points of contention within Potter or the IQA league regarding rules and play?
There aren't any really big points of contention regarding play. Over the past five years we've refined our rules, and hundreds of people around the world now play by them happily. The biggest thing people outside the sport talk about is our human Snitch – we get a decent number of emails from people who think we should use remote-controlled helicopters, or balls buried in the ground, or even, as one emailer suggested, a chicken – but one of the main reasons our version of Quidditch is so popular is the human Snitch.

What is your position on the Broom vs. No Broom controversy?
There are two schools of thought on this: the brooms keep the game magical, closer to its roots, and in a word, a little ridiculous. Quidditch is unlike other competitive college sports in that it doesn't take over your life. Despite using a broom, the game is still very athletic and competitive and takes a lot of skill. The other school of thought is that the sport will never reach the kind of mainstream popularity of other sports because of the broom. I think Quidditch could become – and stay – a very successful niche sport with the brooms. After several years, people have gotten used to it. Most of the teams playing today don't mind the brooms at all.

IQA rules state that teams can't make money off Quidditch (unless it's used for the team or donated to a non-profit), but can individual players be endorsed? Have there been any endorsement deals or sponsorship thus far?
No individual players have been endorsed so far. That would be pretty cool, but I imagine Warner Bros. might have a problem with it, as Quidditch is still its trademark.

Are Muggle versions of Mediwizards present at matches?
All tournaments have trained EMTs present.

Are the majority of injuries broom-related? What are some of the weirdest injuries that have occurred?
Actually, most injuries aren't broom-related. Most injuries are a result of tackling. We've had a broken collarbone, bruised or cracked ribs, sprained ankles...

Has J.K. Rowling ever attended a match?
Not yet, but we would absolutely love to have her!

Are there any broadcasts of the games?
At big tournaments, like the World Cup and official regional tournaments, we live-stream the games to our web site. 20,000 people watched the 2010 World Cup live-stream.

How much support do universities give the league? Are there Quidditch scholarships?
Support varies by school. Some schools, like Chestnut Hill College, are fully funded and endorsed by their university. (To learn more about Chestnut Hill, read the feature on it on pages 17–18 of the February issue of our magazine, The Monthly Seer.) Other teams are club sports or just student clubs or organizations, and some teams get no support from their university at all – either because the

schools don't view Quidditch as a real sport or because it doesn't have a certified referee training program or because it's too physical and too much of a liability. In some cases, schools have convinced their universities. New York University, for example, was denied funding and club sport status because the administration didn't believe Quidditch was a real sport. After NYU competed in the fourth annual Quidditch World Cup, however, and brought back the evidence to the administration, it said there was a very good chance it would be approved as a club sport next year. Even at Middlebury College, the birthplace of Quidditch, it took two years for the sport to be recognized by the university – and that was with a 100-person strong league with 10 intramural teams!

Moorpark College Quidditch in Los Angeles, California, has given out the first Quidditch scholarship, for $25. We haven't heard of schools giving Quidditch scholarships, but the IQA hopes to provide at least one substantial Quidditch scholarship in the next couple of years.

Are there Quidditch summer camps?

There haven't been any dedicated Quidditch summer camps yet, but dozens of camps each summer do offer Quidditch to their participants. They email us to get the rulebook and get questions answered about adapting the rules for younger audiences. The IQA aims to make Quidditch a fixture at even more summer camps this summer.

Can anyone join a Quidditch team? Are there tryouts? What are the logistics for starting teams in your area?

Anyone can join! Tryout procedures differ from team to team. Many teams let anyone and everyone play, but hold tryouts for the competitive team that will travel to tournaments. At Emerson College in Boston, five "house" teams play all year, and a separate World Cup team is formed through tryouts – those players practice throughout the year together as well as in their house teams. Many schools use the house format to form intramural teams, where people sign up to play on Gryffindor, Slytherin, Ravenclaw, or Hufflepuff.

To start a team, you should download the current rulebook from our website for free – or even better, download our handbook for $3, which includes a guidebook with advice on starting a team, making or buying equipment, getting players together for your first game, hosting a tournament, and more. Fill out the "join up" form on the IQA site so an IQA rep in your area can contact you to see if you have any questions and help you get started. Then, find people! Post flyers around school, start a Facebook group, badger your friends, whatever it takes!

We noticed mentions of these in fan fiction; but are there real Quidditch cheerleaders? Mascots?

Chestnut Hill College came to the 2008 World Cup with a saxophone-playing priest for a mascot. It was awesome. The Ursuline School, an all-girls high school in New Rochelle, New York, has a big koala as a mascot, with a Harry Potter scar and glasses. I have yet to see cheerleaders, probably because Quidditch is co-ed, so the girls are playing!

Quidditch seems like a positive co-ed sport. How is the mix between men and women playing? Do you recommend it to fans looking to make compatible love connections?

Apparently, according to Cosmo magazine, Quidditch is a good place to find your next boyfriend! The fact that men and women play together on the Quidditch pitch is actually kind of unremarkable, because it's so normal. The women play with equal ferocity and skill, and as an organization we think co-ed Quidditch is important because it teaches men and women to play with and against each other in a way that doesn't happen in any other college sport. There are many couples who have met on the Quidditch pitch, too.

Have you noticed symptoms of Potter withdrawal within the Quidditch community? How are people dealing with the impending finality of the saga?

I think for the Harry Potter fan, playing Quidditch means not having to let go of the saga. I started reading the books when I was 10, and although nothing will ever replace the decade of eagerly reading and awaiting the next book, look what I get to do for a living! Playing Quidditch allows you to have a connection to the books in a new way, and plus, it's a really fun atmosphere that brings all kinds of people together. When you play Quidditch, you're also part of the Quidditch community – and not just your own team but all Quidditch players.

What are the physical / emotional / mental benefits of Quidditch, particularly for fans of Harry Potter who are possibly experiencing withdrawals?

I guess I started getting to this in the above question. First of all, Quidditch is a very physical activity, and even if you don't really consider yourself athletic, you can play Quidditch! It's a great sport that gets you out there exercising and interacting positively with others, all while making a connection to your favorite book series. For most teams, that camaraderie doesn't end when the Snitch is caught. Teams host parties, read Harry Potter to kids in libraries, have cape-making parties and study parties, movie marathons and canned food drives... in short, Quidditch players become like family. Because you're playing Quidditch for goodness' sake, other Quidditch players are not there to judge you. You get to take part in something ridiculous and awesome and share it with others.

In most sports, hand shakes are the customary way to end the game. Very often in Quidditch, players hug. At the end of the third-place match at the 2010 World Cup, the University of Pittsburgh beat Vassar College in a highly competitive and tense game between two of the best schools in the league. But what did Vassar do after losing third place in the biggest tournament of the year? It converged onto the Pittsburgh team for a giant group hug, and then both teams, led by Vassar, took a victory lap around the pitch, capes flying out behind them, because they were lucky enough to be playing Quidditch, and that's the most important part.

Being a part of Quidditch is magical; I can't think of a better way to describe it.

What do you see as the future of Quidditch?

I think Quidditch will continue to grow in popularity and spread to more and more colleges and high schools around the world. I think there will be more organized tournaments each year, and hopefully even conferences where groups of teams play one another regularly throughout the year. But I also see Quidditch staying accessible to the fans, from those who play casually to those who love Harry Potter. Quidditch has always had the dichotomy of serious, competitive sport and fun, magical activity; and we strive to keep that dichotomy at all times. This year, the World Cup will have two separate divisions, so that teams who play for fun can enjoy the biggest tournament of the year just as much as the team who practiced four days a week and held intense tryouts to battle the top teams in the country.

Essentially, Quidditch is here to stay!

BEST DAY EVER. So, true love on the Quidditch field — not just rumor! Won't get into too much detail, but it's been a long while since I've even liked someone. First I'll say this person is NOT the Snitch (not to sound prejudiced but I have reservations about dating a Snitch — j.k.!). Sure, running around with a broom between one's legs can seem a little bit odd; it's just that there's something quite appealing about it — in a Potteresque sort of way. Sooo, the details — nah, you won't get any out of me. Except to say that Quidditch is the absolutely SEXIEST GAME EVER! And I'm in love!

Chapter Five
Crafting Potter

I LOVE MUGGLE QUIDDITCH! I never ever thought it'd be possible for Muggles to play it without making it lame, but somehow the IQA figured out how to make it cool AND I LOVE IT! The only downer is that I can't join the college team because I'm not a student. There may be a community team, and if there isn't, I'm determined to start one.

Believe it or not, as awesome as it was, the actual match wasn't the best part. The best part was meeting all the people who love Harry Potter as much as I do (some of them even more so), including a few who have been dealing with HPSED, too. After talking to them, I realized that Quidditch is only part of the answer. I mean, I feel sooo much better, but I can't always be on the Quidditch field.

Speaking of the field, that's where I met my true love — yes, match made in Harry heaven — who's not only a major player in the sport but also in the H.P. crafting world. It's kinda awesome. Gorgeous Potterabilia — going to try some myself; hope I can do the crafting world justice!

So my first few tries were takes on something I recall doing as a little kid. Once in the midst of it, though, I started to get this feeling that perhaps my parents' encourage-ment and commentary on my craft-ing projects as a child had been a little blown out of  proportion. Still, I thought they were solid efforts, for my first time around.

My new partner in crime tried to be supportive and kind. There was some mention of donating my Harry and Hedwig pinecones as Christmas ornaments for the needy — not what I was shooting for, but... okay. Pulling myself up by my bootstraps, I considered creating a Mandrake garden but, after buying the seeds, pots and potting soil, I learned this magical and hallucinogenic night-shade, of the species Mandragora officinarum, contains poisonous alkaloids, which can cause coma in cats. So that idea was immediately nixed. (Or should I say nox'ed? Ha-haha.) My next effort was more advanced and included

37

a multitude of sketches for prototypes of real-life flying brooms, incorporated into wall art that I thought would be a great addition to any Harry Potter fan's home decor.

    Though it wasn't meant to be funny, my creation did inspire serious belly laughs, and it was slightly embarrassing when it became a sort of comedy relief during the Sunday afternoon crafting circle. Meanwhile, my love made the coolest Harry paper dolls, which immediately sold on Etsy.

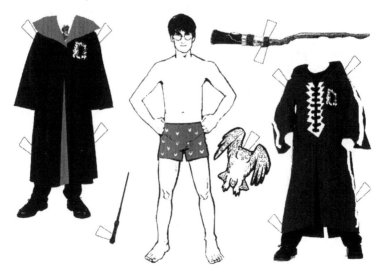

I knew my next foray had to be huge. Something to proclaim my love and redeem my skills. Baking has never been my strong suit, but it does come from the heart, so I approached it as a challenge (and used KungFoodie's Harry Potter Cake as inspiration). Though the first results may have been a little frightening, at least they reflected my feelings for Harry, Quidditch, and the one I loved (not necessarily in that order). It was my version of the Snitch.

Then, I went to my local Salvadorean bakery for inspiration and came up with another version of the Snitch.

I thought I'd at least get an "A for effort." Doesn't the world give out any A's for effort anymore? Considering my lack of musical skills, I should have scored points for not starting a wizard rock band!

I can barely write in you dear Diary, because I'm crumbling right now — just like

my pastries. So many heartfelt crafts and home-baked goodness, and all I got was this note.

I'M SORRY

I CAN'T

DON'T HATE ME —

R.A.B.

P.S. PLEASE STOP MAKING ~~CRAFTS~~

Chapter Six
Analytical Potter

Getting dumped has left me in a really bad space. As awful as I may have felt before, this is the lowest of the low. Thought I was getting better, but maybe I was simply relying on so many outside forces to more or less "distract" rather than help me deal with my issues. Scared it could get worse (especially after noticing a slight case of agoraphobia setting in), I broke down and called a psychoanalyst. I hope I can get myself to the appointment...

I'm Dr. Juana Fuchenstein. What brings you here today?
Anon: I've been diagnosed with Harry Potter Series End Disorder and need to find a way to manage it. I read an article about your history of treating sufferers, and it seemed like you have a pretty high success rate. So, that's why I decided to come see you.

Very good. Now, what would you say is the main problem?
My family and friends think I'm crazy, but I'm not. I actually think

they're crazy for not seeing why I prefer the Wizarding world to the real one. I mean, if you had to choose between a life filled with flying brooms, invisible cloaks, friendly giants, and unicorns or one filled with heinous traffic, skinny jeans, FOX News anchors, and bedbugs, which would you pick? And don't even get me started on their one-dimensional reading material! It just seems like I have nothing in common with anyone around me, which is making me feel really disconnected, kinda like I'm living in a dusty glass bubble. So, I guess you could say all the stuff I just mentioned makes up the main problem. I also can't get "One (Is the Loneliest Number)" by Three Dog Night out of my head, but I don't know if that's related.

I don't think it is. When exactly did you first notice your problem?
"One" constantly playing in my head? A couple of weeks ago. Every now and then it gets replaced by Filter's song from *The X-Files* movie soundtrack, but the original always comes back.

What have other people said? How has that affected you?
That they hate my taste in music. It really doesn't bother me... Oh, you mean regarding Harry Potter. Well, I feel like, somewhere out there, there are people going through the same thing as me. And that eventually we're all going to end up together in a place similar to Hogwarts... but for old people.

Interesting. Now, as you may or may not know, HPSED affects every Potter fan differently. Some experience only mild discomfort while others suffer complete debilitation. Using a scale of A–F, keeping in mind the average length of time you've spent feeling bad, the type of weather patterns, and the moon's size on the day you last felt extremely uncomfortable, what number, from 1 to 10, do you think represents the severity of your withdrawal symptoms?
Six? Maybe seven? I'm a little confused about the scale.

Have you ever been admitted to a psychiatric hospital?
You already think I need to be locked up?

No, no, I simply want to know if you feel you're exhibiting behavior or entertaining thoughts that microchipped Muggles... um... I mean other people might consider odd. Things you may be un-

comfortable talking about.
Well, that's why I came to see you.

Riiiight. Have you seen any other health care professional regarding this problem?
I wanted to see Dr. Harry Potter; his specialty is Internal Medicine focusing on holistic care including mental health, but he's located all the way in Massachusetts and...

Well then, let's move on to medications, shall we? What drugs are you on right now and what drugs have you taken in the past?
Drugs? Normal ones like aspirin and ibuprofen. Some herbal and homeopathic remedies for colds and aches - stuff like that. There were a few concoctions I read about on a Potter forum. I tried to buy a bottle of Essence of Dittany online, which turned out to be catnip extract, which was okay 'cause I have a cat. But no, I've never taken any psychiatric medications.

Good to hear. Now, as far as you know, has anyone in your family suffered from mental illness?
No, no one in my immediate family. Though I do have a cousin who's obsessed with *The Godfather*.

I can understand that. But back to the subject of family - how would you describe your childhood?
It was very happy. I was an only child, so I was spoiled by my parents and grandparents but not in a Veruca Salt kind of way. I have a pretty big family, so there were lots of reunions and outings. Tons of birthday parties, sleepovers, trips to Disneyland... I definitely had a great childhood.

Did you have any serious illnesses or experience any traumatic events while growing up?
None that I can remember.

Which indicates that you did; your subconscious has obviously blocked out your memories. I see it frequently in victims of alien abduction.
Excuse me?

Have you ever heard of The Illuminati?
Ummmm... I don't think so. But can I ask you what...

This is making perfect sense. Now, do you feel you're the only one in control of your thoughts and actions, or are they controlled by someone else?
Wait... what!? You're totally freaking me out right now! Why are you asking me these bizarre questions? And what do aliens have to do with anything?

Calm down. Relaaax. It's necessary that I ask these questions in order to determine the amount of influence J.K. Rowling has on your subconscious mind. You see, I believe there are subliminal messages hidden within her books. For example, you posed this question to me earlier: "...if you had to choose between a life filled with flying brooms, invisible cloaks, friendly giants, and unicorns or one filled with heinous traffic, skinny jeans, FOX News anchors, and bedbugs, which would you pick?"
Yeah. So?

So, what concerns me is that you mentioned flying brooms first.
What?

It's a clear indication of mind control.
What?

You see, it's a well-known fact in certain circles that J.K. Rowling has strong ties to The Illuminati – the true power behind the throne, so to speak. Governments, dictators, kings are all just Mason muppets – The Illuminati are actually the ones manning the control booth of the world. Now I think the Goblet of Fire audiobook Grammy winner Jim Dale is a fracking genius (and I don't mean gas or nuclear), but that doesn't discount the fact that they utilize every avenue of communication to implant ideas into the unconscious mind and have used Rowling to disperse Harry Potter in order to indoctrinate particular segments of the population with occult practices. They initially tried to manipulate the mind of real Muggle Nancy K. Stouffer, of course, but she had too anarchistic a disposition for the coercion to take; and we know how that worked out. Have you gone into the full-body scanners? I hope not! Not only does the C.I.A. own Facebook, it's also in a digital bed with Steve Jobs! You've been tricked into letting them track the "fingerprint" of your talk, your walk, your scent, and every bone in your body through TOS and user agreements! Their mal/spy/stealthware also covertly downloads everything off your cell phone and computer, and (as Bob Woodwand and Carl Bernstin uncovered) even scans and edits full handwritten manuscripts like *The Deathly Hallows*. Have you ever considered why the Fukushima radiation is hitting Hollyweird smack dab in between the last two Potter premieres? Hmmm? Forget GWEN Towers, Chemtrails, HAARP, and warping the ionosphere for militaristic population controlling weather/disaster modification – have you been to the tunnels under Pine Gap? Of course not, because we're not invited to the Club of Rome – bastards! But that's the place to be when the crap hits the fan. Unless you can already travel the ether and tap into the space-time continuum – can you?

Wow, look at the time! I'm going to be late to a meeting if I don't leave now!

Please, hear me out... In the question I cited, you listed flying brooms first. In *The Prisoner of Azkaban*, Harry Potter is given a broom called a "Firebolt" that can pull 7Gs, just like a fighter jet. Now, one of the pioneers in the creation of J.A.T.O (Jet-fuel Assisted Take Off) and the co-founder of Jet Propulsion Laboratory was a man named Jack Parsons. Parsons was also a member of the O.T.O (Ordo Templi Orientis), a secret society led by the notorious occultist Aleister Crowley. And as the O.T.O is a sect of the Order of Illuminati, we finally arrive back to Rowling and your inevitable doom. Now does it all make sense?

Your office validates parking, right?

Wait... don't you want to try hypnosis?

Chapter Seven
Living Potter

As awful as my experience was with Dr. Fuchenstein, I think it was nice of her to follow up with an email.

> "Although an extended period of voluntary commitment is my official recommendation, I would not be opposed to you trying some alternative forms of treatment. If one ignores the blatant promotion of freemasonry, there are Zoroastrianism aspects to the Potter tales that I feel could be of benefit, particularly in regards to the use of knowledge to control your own destiny. Discarding the id is difficult, but one must allow the superego to mature in order to find true altruism. Think of it as a smack in the back by sorcerer Don Juan, or an embrace by Wizard Dumbledore – a gesture that could help transport you beyond the humdrum reality of the Muggle mindset. That said, I believe an organization called the Harry Potter Alliance may be of assistance. They appear to have adopted the positive pro-activism of Dumbledore's Army and could possibly help you find solid mental ground again. They may be your only hope. P.S. If it doesn't work, feel free to call my office to arrange placement at an inpatient facility."

So perhaps she is a psycho psychoanalyst, but I did take her advice to heart. My other option at the time, not to sound too pathetic, was a lawyer who suggested I take legal action (against whom, I'm still unclear). He seemed to think my situation mirrored the one of a Swede who was recently awarded disability for his addiction to Black Sabbath (no really, this actually happened!).

Despite the encouraging headway my lawyer was making in potentially settling out of court for three honorary N.E.W.T.s and a year's supply of Bertie Bott's Every Flavor Beans, it was against my morals to proceed in such a manner. Becoming a ward of the state, so to speak, was equivalent to giving up, and even J.K. endured hardships during those scrappy days as a single mum writing at the coffee shop for goodness sake.

So I decided to stop playing The Order of the Phoenix on my Xbox and started logging onto the forums on a multitude of Harry Potter fan sites instead. No one knows your pain like another experiencing the same.

I started with some fanfic and, considering that the highest grade I ever received in creative writing was a C+, my first foray wasn't that bad:

"If anyone were to say it, even as a joke, he'd punch them in the face. 'I'd rather pal around with that Weasley loser,' thought Draco to himself, 'than snog that disgusting Mudblood Granger.' But why had that idea even popped into his head? It had to be due to the fact that she'd answered every question Professor Binns had asked in the last 10 minutes. After all, how could you NOT notice a bushy-haired know-it-all whose hand was always in the air? She was just asking for it!"

Okay, maybe I got too X-rated with my description of Draco and Hermione subsequently snogging on the Hogwarts Express... but I was trying to be realistic. Helloooo?! Very possible scenario!

After my initial online stumble, I was off and running in the expanse of the worldwide Harry Potter Universe — suddenly rife with opportunities. There were a million strangers with whom I already felt a kinship, who were in a similar boat, and who were there for me, 24 hours a day! From Mugglenet to the Leaky Cauldron to HarryPotter-Latino — how awesome is the Potter community!?!

♡♡♡

"At the end of the day,
the thing that we're all going to have to face —
whether we're Cornelius Fudge or Arthur Weasley —
is Lord Voldemort."

Andrew Slack of
The Harry Potter Alliance

What is it about the Harry Potter story that inspires fans to become activists?

I didn't want to read Harry Potter. I thought it was going to be stupid. All these kids I was working with right out of college kept talking about it and encouraging me to read it, and I just thought "Okay, I'll try it" (this was Halloween 2002), and I picked up the first book. I had been yearning to go back to college, the campus experience, and I found that campus in Hogwarts; I found something that I just didn't expect. [Activism] is intrinsic to the entire story, from the very beginning, from the very first sentence: *"Mr. and Mrs. Dursley, of number four, Privet Drive, were proud to say that they were perfectly normal, thank you very much."*

And then it continues. They wouldn't want to be caught up in anything strange or mysterious; then it makes allusions to the Potters. And I just started laughing out loud through that entire chapter. Mr. Dursley selling drills and yelling at people and this sort of rat race that J.K. Rowling's indicting that's all about spying on your neighbors while you're living this very petty sort of existence that I refer to as the "Muggle Mindset," where the ideal is perfect normalcy, thank you very much.

There's a subversive quality to the book the second it starts. The first thing in the book is subversive because she is sarcastically, satirically suggesting norms are not necessarily good. And that's a premise of all social activism: What's considered normal is not necessarily a good thing. But she goes deeper than a lot of activists would do in terms of economic injustice, or various kinds of injustices – she goes into the strange and mysterious. She goes into attitudes and behaviors beyond structure. As the books progress, she ends up [dissecting] the structural elements of the Wizarding World, and we begin to see a tremendous amount of corruption.

In book two, we're introduced to the concept of racism and how it's wrong. We begin to understand that this "Muggle Mindset" of valuing normalcy exists [beyond] people like the Dursleys. Hermione's family are Muggles and they are good people; they're nice, good dentists that encourage her as a wizard (I use that as a gender-neutral term). But in the Wizarding World, there's also a type of "Muggle Mindset" that values normalcy. And the normalcy that is valued is that Muggle-born wizards are not equal to "Pure Blood" wizards and that the Muggle World is inferior to the Wizarding World. And in the third book, we are introduced to the concept that Dementors are used in prisons, and Dumbledore is against this. He's against prison torture, which is connected to a sort of activist cause that we again see in the third book. Sirius has been arrested in a time of terror when habeas corpus was suspended. He wasn't given a trial; he was tortured for 13 years [though he] was innocent. And this is very, very similar to a lot of the issues that I imagine J.K. Rowling dealt with at Amnesty International (and that the U.S. was dealing with at the time, coincidentally).

And this progresses into the end of the fourth book with Voldemort returning and Dumbledore saying, "Look, we need to get rid of the Dementors. We need to send envoys to the Giants because it's essential that we have diplomacy and unity and no longer consider them an inferior group even if they are different and dysfunctional – at least for the time being. And we need to stop looking at purity of blood as the most important thing."

And Cornelius Fudge, the minister, dismisses all these ideas as preposterous, including the thesis of the idea that Voldemort has returned, and we need to respond to that. So, within the fifth book, that's where the activism really sets in, in a structural way. As the media, which is totally consolidated, and the government continues to deny and drag its feet even in the face of overwhelming evidence that Voldemort is back, they hold

> ## *Why don't we become a* **Dumbledore's Army** *for the real world?*

onto this idea that Voldemort is not back, [and] it's up to Harry and his friends to start an underground activist group, Dumbledore's Army, to wake the world up to the fact that Voldemort is back – and they are successful in doing that. As I read that, I believed it was time for Harry Potter fans, who spend so much of our talent, our energy, and our resources on Harry Potter sites, engaged in Harry Potter music, engaged in Harry Potter fan fiction. Why don't we think about being like the characters? Why don't we become a Dumbledore's Army for the real world and wake our governments and our Daily Prophets up to things that need to be done and that are tantamount to Voldemort returning. Things like the climate crisis, [which] we're not even dealing with. We're still questioning if the Dark Lord (i.e., climate crisis) even exists.

Regardless of who we want to blame, there is a strong movement within the country to deny reality in what is arguably still the most powerful country in the world, and it's absurd. So, my first post about this in 2006... Harry and the Potters (Paul and Joe DeGeorge), who co-founded this organization with me, they sent out a post about the climate crisis with me, comparing it to Voldemort returning.

Anyone that wants to stand in the way of fighting the climate crisis at this point is insignificant. They're as insignificant as Cornelius Fudge or Dolores Umbridge. They're puny, they're pathetic, and they're incredibly dangerous. At the end of the day, the thing that we're all going to have to face – whether we're Cornelius Fudge or Arthur Weasley – is Lord Voldemort. It is the climate crisis itself, and the price is much higher than having to deal with someone annoying like Fudge, who's quasi-totalitarian. The price is going to be the lives of millions of people. And that's something that even activists don't bring up very often, but the human cost of this crisis is pretty undeniable and has already begun, and it's going to get so much worse. I think "dark and difficult times," in Dumbledore's words, would be an understatement. But Dumbledore tends to be understated... because he's British.

With dark forces on all sides, how does an organization like HPA – and the many fans – figure out how to focus their energies?
It's been a very organic process. And it's been a combination of me and a handful of people deciding things and responding to our members. It's a really ongoing process of figuring out the best way to do it. We don't want to be a dictatorship in any sense of the word and come up with how people should think and do things. But on the other end, there needs to be some sort of degree of getting stuff done and creating campaigns and initiatives, so it's really been a balancing act.

Awesome *is the only force in the world that can fight "world suck."*

In the beginning, the main issue was around Darfur. Part of the reason was that I started the organization with Paul [DeGeorge], and it was an issue we both felt passionately about. I'd just seen *Hotel*

Rwanda and it really, really flipped me out because I'm Jewish and around the age of 10, I just became enamored with Holocaust movies. My mom and I would sit and watch so many of them. And I had no idea that when I was 14 and *Schindler's List* was in the middle of winning Best Picture that a genocide was going on and killing more than a million people and could have been prevented. Or at least those numbers could have been brought down significantly. So, there are a lot of problems in the world – as Nerdfighters would say. Do you know the Nerdfighters?

No.
Well, we'll talk about that later. But there's a significant amount of "world suck." Nerdfighters say that, as nerds, we aren't made of bone, tissue, or muscle like most people are made up of. We're made of the force of awesome, and awesome is the only force in the world that can fight "world suck." So it's a very amorphous "being against badness" and then thinking, "How do you tackle that?"

I didn't bring up LGBTQ equality, but when it comes to gay rights, there are a lot of members who are gay. I think if you look at children, the first thing a child understands when it comes to activism is litterbugs. It's the most obvious thing, at least with a privileged child – they don't like litter. But then when you get into teenage-hood, a lot of teenagers in this day and age have the need to come out of the closet or have friends who are coming out of the closet, and they've been exposed to enough media about that that equality is a major issue for them. Unfortunately, for a lot of white Americans there might not be enough equality around Latinos and Muslims as there needs to be. So, for the LGBTQ stuff, we have Hagrid having to hide in the closet for his identity as a half-giant; Lupin having to hide in the closet for being a werewolf; Harry Potter literally forced to live inside a closet for the first 11 years of his life; and we want to create environments as Dumbledore wanted to create environments that are conducive to no one having to live in the closet for their identity – be it for their race, their gender, their ethnicity, creed, or sexual orientation or gender identification. So, we work on that issue and that has gotten a huge response, so we continue to go back to that issue.

To answer your question, the response has been so amazing. As well as the one we've had toward literacy. Literacy wasn't one of my number-one issues, but it's certainly one of the things in this community that gets people really fired up – giving books to people in need.

Is that the Accio Books campaign?
Exactly. We introduced that two years ago, and it was something that brought so much life back into the organization – people just got so into it. And we divided things into houses just like in Harry Potter. You get points according to how many books you're donated. We had heads of houses at the time. We had Evanna Lynch (who plays Luna Lovegood) as head of Ravenclaw, and that brought life into things and people were really excited and remain really excited about Accio Books. I'm really excited about Accio Books.

The trick is that we want to have really intelligent activists, wizarding activists; so, that said, we have a situation where we want people to have that experience of giving their books that they love to somebody else. That wonderful form of charity and partnership with other individual human beings, and doing things like Helping Haiti Heal where we're taking their money and raffling off amazing prizes. We raised over $123K in two weeks thanks to an alliance between us and the Nerdfighters as well as over 20 other fan communities and a bunch of best-selling young adult authors and J.K. Rowling, all who gave the prizes that were raffled off. That's how we raised that money and were able to send five cargo planes to

Haiti that were full of medical supplies – four of them named after Harry Potter characters and one of them named DFTBA, which is the Nerdfighters' slogan, "Don't Forget to be Awesome." And in that instance, the choice of organization was Partners In Health, which is another relief organization. The reason we chose this organization is because they've been in Haiti for over 20 years and have a very, very strong anti-poverty agenda. They work with the government, and that's sort of the great microcosm of what we're trying to do.

Which is, yes, charity. Yes, giving money. Yes, giving books. But also thinking about long-term change. And doing advocacy that involves actions such as calling 1-800-Genocide, which was created by our partners, the Genocide Intervention Network. We really want people to have a complex and nuanced view of activism.

The Deathly Hallows campaign has been designed as such. Just about every month, we're putting out a different Horcrux, and by the end, we're going to have a kind of dissertation of sorts that can show how World Suck works; or how Voldemort works. How all these different issues, the Dementor Horcrux and the Body Bind Horcrux, are obviously related because our sense of physical empowerment combined with depression, anxiety, and different emotions and how we process emotions are obviously connected. But it's also connected in that, if we have disempowered people physically and emotionally as a population, we're not going to be thinking much about the chocolate we eat. Because the chocolate we eat matters and it matters in big ways. And that's why we're asking for all Harry Potter chocolate to be fair trade.

And that's the Not In Harry's Name campaign?

Exactly. We just had Evanna Lynch sign a petition for that, and we're going to have more celebrities sign. Warner Bros. has been responsive. The [chocolate] company has an "F" from one of our partner groups in terms of their ethics when it comes to the chocolate trade. The ramifications of that are huge. For one, cocoa farmers are starving regardless of the fact that they're given wages – starvation wages. For two, the chocolate trade is full of child slaves who are kidnapped from their families and abused in situations of slavery. And number three, cocoa farmers are wising up and finding other crops besides cocoa to make money so that they can live. And they're doing it at such a fast rate that if it continues, according to a study that was done last year, in 20 years chocolate will be as rare and as expensive as caviar. So that's how it's all connected.

We see how violence is connected as well. When we support companies that invest in other companies that then invest in the government of Sudan, [they're supporting] genocide. And it's a problem that I'm wrestling with, because I happen to be very close with a company that has a billion dollars in Petro-China, which is one of the underwriters of the genocide in Darfur. So we're looking at the complex way the issues interact. So, unlike a values-based organization that fights genocide or fights poverty or sexism or homophobia or what have you, we're an organization that looks at the whole picture in order to educate a community not simply in a cursory way where we're taking a tour of social injustice but, instead, looking at these issues deeply and their connections.

What is J.K. Rowling's feedback on your organization? You said you worked with her on one of your campaigns?

Well, the first interaction I ever had with her was through Melissa Anelli, who is on our board and who runs the Leaky Cauldron. She took a letter I had written to J.K. at the end of November. I was so nervous writing this letter, and I was crying when I wrote it. It was really emotional and scary to tell her about what we were doing, because we'd been doing it for years and had put so much heart and soul into it that I'd [have been] upset if she didn't like it. And Melissa said that she'd already heard of us. She gave the letter to J.K. Rowling in her house, and she said she'd already heard of us and she smiled and seemed really receptive. And then she read the letter and said something like "God bless him" or something like that, and then she said she was going to write a letter back to me. But before that happened, *Time* happened to ask her about us and she flipped out. And it was in *Time* when they named her the second runner-up as person of the year. I can send you the quote where she just flips out and says how humbled she is, and she put it on her website and it's still there. We were the most recent fan site to be given an award on her website – this was at the end of 2007 – and it was just wonderful. It was a great honor. She said we were like Dumbledore's Army, and that's exactly what we wanted to be. And she sent a letter to my house saying that we were the purest expression of the spirit of Dumbledore within the Harry Potter fandom, and that she was humbled and excited to be associated with it in any way. She helped us with Helping Haiti Heal and donated the seven signed Harry Potter books. That's been about the extent of it, but it's been wonderful and really positive.

That's really awesome.

These are excellent questions, and I really want to talk to you more about this idea of myth-based activism. Because, if you look at a religion, you'll see that it doesn't pick just one issue. And we're not a religion. We don't deify anyone in these books; we're part of a fandom. But the only way a fandom is similar to a religion is that it's an organized group of people or decentralized, either way, that is united by their love of a story or stories. And so, in that regard, there is a sort of similarity, but in every other regard, there's no sense of religious worship of Dumbledore that's done publicly every Friday night or every Sunday morning. I mean, that would be kind of interesting... but we're

There's no sense of religious worship of Dumbledore that's done publicly every Friday night or every Sunday morning. **I mean, that would be kind of interesting...** *but we're not advocating for that.*

not advocating for that. So, you can't be authentic to a story if you just pick one issue. I mean, you can, but that wasn't what we aimed to do. We aimed to be a Dumbledore's Army that's not only making an external impact on these issues but has three goals.

One: To make an external impact, whether it's on people in Haiti or the LGBTQ issues or refugees or what have you.

Two: To empower a community of Harry Potter fans to be educated as sophisticated and engaged activists and organizers in our world with a far more sophisticated and deep understanding of activism than most activists. If they focus on one issue later on in their lives, great; they'll do it with a greater sense of imagination, of art and the use of social media and how the issues are connected and a greater sense of self, hopefully. There's a tremendous story that we have about the self-esteem of our members, their friendships, the relationships that have been formed within the Harry Potter Alliance.

Three: Bring to activism a sense of innovation – a sense of playfulness and fun that we don't see and to bring to literature and popular culture a sense of innovation and seriousness in terms of its applicability to real world issues.

You mentioned you worked with other fan communities for the HPA's "Helping Haiti Heal" campaign. Was that experience what inspired you to create the Imagine Better Coalition?
Long before the Harry Potter Alliance, I wanted to create an organization and be part of leading a movement that dealt with the arts and story for social change. I made many attempts at beginning this, and it never caught on until I was encouraged by a friend to blog about Harry Potter, which I did. And then I kept blogging about it because Harry was like my passion and it was all I would talk about. I go through phases, and Harry was a phase that was not going away. And I just began thinking, "You know, we should turn this into an organization" – which is when I introduced myself to Harry and the Potters and we started the organization together. As it grew, I began thinking, "Wow, we are starting a base of people across the world that's like a real-life constituency that has committed to the ideas of stories for social change." So, in essence, the Harry Potter Alliance was an accident for me that ended up going to where we're going now; my original wish, which is really exciting.

As an actual fan of the Harry Potter books, my most profound loss already came in 2007. That's when I received *Harry Potter and the Deathly Hallows.* I held that book, completely overwhelmed that the story was coming to an end. Oftentimes I would actually start to get angry at the book, for I knew with each turn of the page, I was nearing the stories completion. And I didn't want to say goodbye to my friends at Hogwarts. I knew I could always go to them in my heart, but up until that time, I always had more adventures to look forward to directly from their creator, J.K. Rowling. Now I know I can still go to them. It's not exactly the same as it was before 2007, there is certainly a loss. But from that loss, I have grown as an individual. I have been inspired to bring my friends from Hogwarts with me into the world in new ways and to some degree, to do it on my own. In the end, we all must take that walk into the Forbidden Forest alone, as Harry does in the infamous Chapter 34 of *Deathly Hallows.* But even then, we're not alone. Even then, Harry was not alone. He

was surrounded and supported by Sirius, Lupin, his dad, and most of all, his mum. They were with him, guarding him, protecting him, allowing his weakened body to walk through a crowd of Dementors, acting as a collective Patronus. And they encouraged him to put down his wand, and realize that his true power was in his ability to stand before Voldemort, vulnerable and from that place of vulnerability, he would cross the other side of the barrier of Platform Nine and Three-quarters, end up in King's Cross station, and be invited on a new journey. But Dumbledore is there to let him know that he's not ready for this new journey. He still must return. Harry Potter ending was not my death. I still needed to return to the world. And that's what I've done since I finished that last book. And I have been surrounded by my friends at Hogwarts. And standing with them have been friends from all the stories I have ever loved, supporting me. It's lonely, yes. But in some ways, it's the least lonely I can possibly be, standing with all of my friends from the stories that I adore, the friends that I adore. There are those who would claim that I am under some illusion. That these characters are only in my head. But as Dumbledore would say, of course it's only happening in my head – but why on earth should that mean it isn't real?

Helping Haiti Heal was the first real opportunity to enact the vision I had a long time ago. And so we went into high gear, and it brought together all these young adult authors and over 20 fan communities, and it showed that the model we are doing [the Imagine Greater Coalition] can work.

Have you witnessed any signs of Harry Potter Series-End Disorder? What is your advice to someone who might be feeling H.P. withdrawal symptoms?
I recognize that the Harry Potter fandom since 2007 has had the movies as a unifying factor – and the fact that the last movie stimulates a significant change. No longer will Harry be in the zeitgeist

of culture the way he has been for so long. We'll need to find new adventures and journeys – and already I'm seeing plenty of Harry Potter fans doing that as Nerdfighters and fans of Dr. Who. Moreover, I'm seeing them take the characters they know and love and the friends in the fandom and going beyond the contours of this one particular moment in movie making and for that matter, Harry Potter history. But Harry will always be there, waiting for us, for another adventure both in our heads and still in those books.

It is true, and this can't be denied, that the experience of Wizard Rock, fan sites, podcasts and livestreams, fan art, fan fiction, role play, Harry Potter Alliance, conferences and more have allowed, as Paul [DeGeorge] would say, the solitude of reading to become a communal experience. That's why with the Harry Potter Alliance, we started Imagine Better. We don't want to see an end to that communal experience and the power that that communal experience has to renew both our souls as individuals and the soul of our collective world and humanity. That is why we have already begun working with fan communities of other blockbuster books, TV shows, and movies (while remaining committed to Harry Potter) as well as the world's most prominent YouTube celebrities and NYT best selling authors in an unprecedented network that takes a bottom up approach toward harnessing the energy of modern myth, social media, and popular culture for social change.

Harry Potter is the most popular piece of fiction in human history. That is how we began this journey of using story to change the world. And we will stay committed to the values within that journey. But it is only our beginning; our moment of landing in Oz. Now we leave the Munchkin City and begin this adventure anew, always knowing that the power to return to home is right at our feet.

In short, while people may be freaking out that this is the end of an era, it's also the start of a new one. The two are very much connected. And the Harry Potter Alliance and Imagine Better will work to ensure that transition takes place in a way that feels empowering, safe, adventurous, and awesome.

Conclusion

Despite all the ups and downs, this has been an amazing learning experience. I now realize that I'm not really saying goodbye to Harry Potter. True, there may be no more books or movies, but Harry can live on in other ways. I may still be an addict — but I've turned it into something positive. Now I simply call it a lifestyle — and an altruistic one at that! The fan sites (and the fans themselves) have shown me that there is a broader scope on which to focus my devotion. Who cares if my crafting sucks or if I never eat another chocolate frog? (Actually, I'd kill right now for one of those tasty reptiles.) What's important is that my love for Harry is not the source of sadness anymore, it's a jumping-off point. Okay, so I may be the one behind the petition to force J.K. to scribe the prequel (and I'll happily indulge in Pottermore with the rest of Rowling's Army.) but all of that's just icing. Because, as it now stands, my Harry Potter-infused life is pretty darn sweet.

Help!

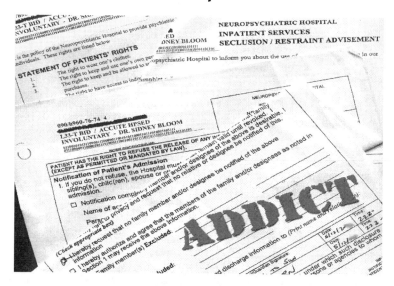

Bloody hell! I managed to wriggle out of the restraints and am now hiding in the basement of St. Mungo's Hospital for Magical Maladies and Injuries and writing this before they find me. Listen – this is the REAL me! The REAL author of the diary. Somehow, these two girls, Kerin and Darby, and some group of quacks called the Potternium Remedium Consortium, managed to get their hands on my diary, then had me locked up in the closed ward and are publishing it as a positive self-help book. WTF?!? I'm not allowed to use the phone so there's no way of contacting anyone to let them know what's really going on. Don't believe a single word of it. There's no happy ending! There's no silver-lined Harry Potter cloud! Please, whatever you do, I beg of you, DO NOT TURN THE PAGE! There's a monster... I mean a Wizard at the end of this book!

Whatever you do, do not turn the...

It All Ends Here

Resources

This book would not have been possible without the help of the Harry Potter fan community. To find a detailed list of sites, organizations and other Harry Potter-related rescources, please visit our blog: **anonymouspotteraddict.word-press.com.**

About Us

Darby Romeo and Kerin Morataya are accomplished players in the pop-culture world. Darby created the landmark punk/music/culture magazine *Ben Is Dead* and has contributed to *Vanity Fair*, *The Village Voice Literary Supplement*, and *Los Angeles Times*; she also edited Lollapalooza's tour magazine. Overwhelmed with her success (ahem!), she sold her worldly possessions and ran away to an island. Today she spends her days catching waves, opening coconut husks with her teeth (with the help of her dog) and running the popular wahine surf/culture/eco site Coconut Girl Wireless. If someone calls her Wilkie she will respond.

Kerin has contributed articles to *Vanity Fair*, *Raygun*, *Playboy*, *Elle* and was a major force behind *Ben Is Dead*. After doing time in the music industry, she moved to Chicago and became an art director at a couple of trade publications you've probably never heard of. She now resides in LA, works on a variety of collaborative creative projects (with the help of her cat) and hopes to one day become a contestant on *Cash Cab*. Oh and she once got stoned with 2-Pac. Admit it, you're jealous.

Together, Darby and Kerin created the *I Hate Brenda Newsletter* and founded the band Rump. Whether or not they were intoxicated at the time is pure speculation. They've appeared on everything from CNN to *The People's Court*. Little Brown published an offshoot book from editions of *Ben Is Dead* entitled *Retro Hell: Life in the '70s and '80s from Afros to Zotz*. While both zines are defunct, The UCLA Arts Library has permanently installed The Darby Romeo Collection of Zines, housing a selection of some of the best publications from the '80-'90s underground 'zine movement. Today, Kerin and Darby are not-so-anonymous Harry Potter addicts, coming to terms with life after Hogwarts.

Credits

COVER ART
Kerin Morataya and Darby Romeo

ACTION POTTER
IQA Action Shot 1 by Kate Olen; IQA Action Shot 2 by Jim Kiernan

CRAFTING POTTER
Knitted Hedwig by Lucy Ravenscar
Salvadorean Snitch Cake photo by KRK
Broom Art/Prototype by Victor Morataya, Morataya Mundo Inventions Corp.

LIVING POTTER
Film Strip Photos 1 courtesy Partners in Health; Film Strip Photos 2 by Kelly Danver

ALL OTHER ART
Title Page "Tear & Glasses"; Prologue "Host Family"; Introduction "H.P. Nightmare"; Chapter One "HPSED Patches"; Chapter Two "APA Flyer"; Chapter Three "Wizarding World Receipts", "Bank Statement"; Chapter Four "Quidditch as per Lakers Playbook"; Chapter Five "Potter Pine Cones", "Potter Paper Dolls", "Snitch Cookie", "Harry & the City Break-up Note"; Chapter Six "Dr. Aleister"; Chapter Seven "HPA Film Strips"; Help! "Involuntary Addict"; Conclusion "Mended Heart"; It All Ends Here "VATEOTB" by Kerin Morataya Introduction "H.P. Nightmare"; Chapter Seven "Desktop"; Harry Potter Addict Emporium advertisement by Darby Romeo

PROOFREADER
Dave "Super Copy Editor" Baker (any errors were added after we got the copy back)

ePUB SCARINESS
Darby Romeo, Convert A Book and BookBaby

BOOK LAYOUT
Kerin Morataya

Made in the USA
Lexington, KY
31 May 2015